ASK MR. BEAR

STORY AND PICTURES

BY

MARJORIE FLACK

Macmillan/McGraw-Hill School Publishing Company
New York ▪ Chicago ▪ Columbus

Macmillan/McGraw-Hill School Division
10 Union Square East
New York, New York 10003

Printed in the United States of America
ISBN 0-02-179472-3 / 1, L.1-5A

  2 3 4 5 6 7 8 9 WES 99 98 97 96 95 94 93

ASK MR. BEAR

Once there was a boy named Danny.
One day Danny's mother had a birthday.
Danny said to himself,
     "What shall I give
          my mother
              for her
                 birthday?"

So Danny started out to see what he could find.
He walked along, and he met a Hen.
"Good morning, Mrs. Hen,"
said Danny.
"Can you give me
    something for
    my mother's
    birthday?"

"Cluck, cluck," said the Hen. "I can give you
a nice fresh egg for your mother's birthday."
"Thank you," said Danny, "but she has an egg."
"Let's see

what we

can find then,"

said the Hen.

So Danny and the Hen

skipped along   until they met

a Goose.

"Good morning, Mrs. Goose," said Danny.

"Can you give me
    something for
    my mother's
    birthday?"

"Honk, honk," said the Goose. "I can give you
some nice feathers to make a fine pillow
for your mother's birthday."
"Thank you," said Danny, "but she has a pillow."
        "Let's see

                what we

                        can find then,"

                                said the Goose.

So Danny

and the Hen

and the Goose

all hopped along until they met

a Goat.

"Good morning, Mrs. Goat," said Danny.

"Can you give me

something

for my mother's

birthday?"

"Maa, maa," said the Goat. "I can give you milk for making cheese."

"Thank you," said Danny, "but she has some cheese."

"Let's see

what we can find then,"

said the Goat.

So Danny and the Hen and the Goose

and the Goat all galloped along until they met

a Sheep.

"Good morning, Mrs. Sheep," said Danny.

"Can you give me something

for my mother's birthday?"

"Baa, baa," said the Sheep. "I can give you some wool to make a warm blanket for your mother's birthday."

"Thank you," said Danny, "but she has a blanket."

"Let's see what we can find then," said the Sheep.

So Danny and the Hen and the Goose

and the Goat and the Sheep
all trotted along until they met

a Cow.

"Good morning, Mrs. Cow," said Danny. "Can you give me something for my mother's birthday?"

"Moo, moo," said the Cow. "I can give you some milk and cream."

"Thank you," said Danny, "but she has some milk and cream."

"Then ask Mr. Bear," said the Cow.
"He lives in the woods over the hill."

"All right," said Danny. "Let's go and ask Mr. Bear."

"No," said the Hen.

"No," said the Goose.

"No," said the Goat.

"No," said the Sheep.

"No — no," said the Cow.

So Danny went alone to find Mr. Bear.

He ran and he ran until he came to the hill, and

he walked and he walked
until he came to the woods, and

there he met—

Mr. Bear.

"Good morning, Mr. Bear," said Danny. "Can you give me something for my mother's birthday?"

"Hum, hum," said the Bear. "I have nothing to give you for your mother's birthday, but I can tell you something you can give her."

So Mr. Bear
whispered a secret
in Danny's ear.
"Oh," said Danny.
"Thank you,
Mr. Bear!"

Then he ran through the woods and he skipped down the hill and he came to his house.

"Guess what I have for your birthday!"
Danny said to his mother.

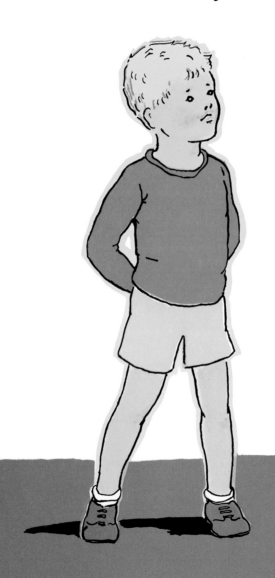

So his mother tried to guess.

"Is it an egg?"

"No, it isn't an egg," said Danny.

"Is it a pillow?"

"No, it isn't a pillow," said Danny.

"Is it a cheese?"

"No, it isn't a cheese," said Danny.

"Is it a blanket?"

"No, it isn't a blanket," said Danny.

"Is it milk or cream?"

"No, it isn't milk or cream," said Danny.

His mother could not guess at all. So—

Danny gave his mother
a Big Birthday
Bear Hug.